W9-BUK-167

5
-minute
mysteries
by MICHAEL AVALLONE
Cases from the Files of Ed Noon, Private Eye

JOHN A. LESLIE
LIBRARY
SCARBOROUGH

SCHOLASTIC BOOK SERVICES
New York Toronto London Auckland Sydney Tokyo

For the man who was first a fan,
then a friend, then ultimately
a champion and prime historian of
The Life and Hard Times of Ed Noon—
Stephen Mertz. I wish there were
ten more like him.

No part of this publication may be reproduced in whole
or in part, or stored in a retrieval system, or transmitted
in any form or by any means, electronic, mechanical,
photocopying, recording, or otherwise, without written
permission of the publisher. For information regarding
permission, write to Scholastic Book Services, 50 West
44th Street, New York, NY 10036.

ISBN: 0-590-05368-X

Copyright © 1978 by Michael Avallone. All rights re-
served. Published by Scholastic Book Services, a division
of Scholastic Magazines, Inc.

16 15 14 13 12 11 10   1 2 3/8

A Word to the Reader

These Ed Noon stories are adapted from scripts I wrote for a long-running radio series of the 50's called *The Windup*.

Ed Noon isn't your garden variety of private detective. He doesn't beat up punks and he's not a brutal slob with a judge-jury-executioner chip on his shoulder. Ed Noon is a human being.

Ed Noon also uses his head! He doesn't climb all over the police department, thumbing his nose at law and order. Neither does he clobber innocent bystanders. He's simply a good guy to have in your corner when trouble comes your way. A private eye with heart, and guts, and brains.

Michael Avallone

Thirteen Riddles

and THIRTEEN SOLUTIONS —
provided by you and Ed Noon.

Riddle One:
The French Jewel Heist

Reading Time: 4 minutes, 10 seconds

Hint:
Benjamin Franklin's kite in a storm.

Hi, this is Ed Noon. I'm here to test you out as a detective. You'll have a chance to solve the crime along with me. Come on, now. See if you can be in at <u>The Windup.</u>

Winding up the French Case was like telling time without a clock. There was so little to go by.

For one thing, the French Shop on Fifth Avenue, a jewelry store second only to Tiffany's in the selling of expensive ice, had been picked as clean as a new whistle of a display full of emeralds and diamonds worth more than three hundred and fifty thousand bucks. The haul had been pulled off after-hours while Manhattan was sleeping.

Only Jeff de Ryn, one of the store owners, and John Fletcher, the night watchman, had been on the premises after closing time. Ryn had been going over the books in his third-floor office. His two partners, Jay Foster and Henry Ball, were away in Chicago at a jewelers' convention. The cops were pretty sure it was an inside job. For very good reasons:

Somebody had known how to take the

teeth out of the burglar alarm set-up, cut off the main electrical power in the building, and perform the robbery without disturbing Mr. de Ryn. Fletcher the night watchman had been asleep in the basement. A half-empty pint of cheap rye on the floor had been proof enough that he had been drinking — and sleeping on the job. The cops held him for questioning and although Fletcher had been with the French Shop all of twenty years, de Ryn could not see how the store could have been rifled without his help.

The missing ice didn't turn up and with the Law making very little headway, I wasn't surprised when Jay Foster, one of de Ryn's partners, hired me to see what I could come up with.

"You see, Mr. Noon," Foster told me, "I do not completely trust Mr. de Ryn or Mr. Henry Ball. They may be my partners but a man can't be too careful when it comes to three hundred and fifty thousand dollars, can he?"

"No, he can't," I agreed. "You have any clues?"

"Well, Ball was with me in Chicago when the crime was committed, of course. But that doesn't mean anything — a man can hire accomplices while he provides himself with an alibi."

I couldn't say no to that either, but I didn't trust any of the three partners, including the man who was hiring me. That's an old trick too, to divert suspicion away from one's self.

When I'm working on a case, I can't afford to trust my own mother. There is simply no other way for a good detective to be.

So I went to work right away.

And came up with some very important, key facts:

Like — *A* — Henry Ball's personal finances were none too good. He was a bad gambler and some of the worst crooks in town were holding his I.O.U.'s.

And — *B* — Jeff de Ryn collected paintings and owned one of the finest private collections in the U.S. of A. It was rumored he had once shelled out forty thousand peas for a small Van Gogh item.

C. Jay Foster was currently married for the third time and was deep in alimony's waves.

Conclusion?

They all needed fresh money.

Robbing your own jewelry store might just be what the doctor ordered.

My next move was to interview all three of them, one at a time, apart from each other. I saw Mr. de Ryn first.

4

"Mr. Noon, I assure you I looked for Fletcher after I was done with the book-keeping. All of twenty minutes, in fact. Then I took the private elevator on my floor down to the basement. Imagine how I felt to find our night watchman drunk and sound asleep. No wonder he didn't hear the burglars."

Jay Foster was equally as informative. "Certainly, our jewelry is insured against theft, Noon. Yes, and de Ryn and Ball and I are all equal partners. It's been that way since we opened French's."

Henry Ball proved to be the one who had supervised the installation of the burglary-alarm system. As he also told me, "Fletcher can't be the one. He's just an old drunk we kept on the job out of sympathy. I think a gang of crooks has been casing the store for months and finally made a score on the right night, that's all. You ask Fletcher, he must have seen someone loitering these past few days —— " Ask Fletcher I did. I had to ask him in jail where he was cooling off his heels as the Number One Suspect.

Fletcher proved to be a poor old slob victimized by the circumstances. "Tell me what happened," I suggested.

"I had a couple too many, Mr. Noon. But even drunk I do what I have to do about my work, that is. There I was, down in the basement, trying to get the electrical current back on. Them thieves sure put it out of order. Then, Mr. de Ryn found me, kinda passed out on my cot — "

Well, there it was. The solution.

When I told the police all I knew, they pulled the Real Man in and he broke down under a strong grilling. He'd needed money, all right, and because of one tiny slip, he would have had it just the way he wanted it.

If you've been reading carefully, you'd know who engineered The French Jewel Heist.

THE SOLUTION:

It had to be Jeff de Ryn.

Who else?

If the electrical power had been shut off as he claimed it was, for the theft had been accomplished while he was upstairs, doing his books, *he could never have taken an elevator down to the basement to look for Fletcher.* Not unless he was a magician.

Elevators still run on electricity.

They did the last time I rode in one. Therefore, he was lying.

And one lie always leads to a bigger one; in this case, four trays of hot ice that would have netted a fortune when properly fenced. So the French Diamond Robbery made all the papers and I was in at *The Windup.*

You were too, if you were reading and thinking properly.

Riddle Two:
The Coronet Club Caper

Reading Time: 4 minutes, 31 seconds

Hint:
**What was the color of
George Washington's white horse?**

Ed Noon at you again. Listen very carefully to all the clues. You'll have the
whole case in less than five minutes. On
your toes, now.

Benny Ricco wanted to see me.

In view of the fact that Benny is one
of the biggest racketeers in Little Old
New York, he generally gets what he
wants. I drove over to his fancy nightclub in thirty minutes flat and had the
questionable pleasure of having Slugger,
his biggest and toughest bruiser, usher
me into the back office where Benny was
waiting for me. Benny is pretty nice
as racketeers go, because he doesn't kill
people or slap anyone around to get ahead
in the world. He's a legal crook whose
fortune comes out of shrewd bookmak-
ing and policy rackets. You know — people who bet on numbers. Anyway, Benny
was glad to see me and he poured me a
Scotch-on-the-rocks while he told me the
reason for his summons. It seemed the
Coronet Club had had a robbery!

"This will hand you a laugh, Noon,

but the safe on the wall there behind that genuine Van Gogh has been rifled of close to one hundred thousand bucks. I'm heartbroken, pal. It has to be an inside job — one of my own gang. For one thing, the dough is a collection of policy money so I can't call the Law in. They wouldn't exactly sympathize. For another, it's very hard for me to think that one of my own kind is a cheap chiseler. I've been good to all of them. Like a father."

"Are you the only one who knows the combination to the safe?" I asked Benny.

"Just me and Slugger. And I trust him like he was my own son."

"Which leaves who else, Benny?"

He sighed, smiling. "Well, you know me and the ladies. I always had an eye for a pretty one. There are three I'm keeping company with now and they *do* come and go as they please."

"Okay," I said. "Trot them in. They must be here now or you wouldn't have been in such a hurry to get me over here."

Benny Ricco chuckled, pressed a buzzer on his desk, and Slugger marched right in with three lovely ladies in tow. The women were pouting and indignant that good old Benny obviously didn't trust them, but I knew how Benny felt. If he had been a Capone, he would have beat the truth out of them. But like I said, he was a businessman. No rough stuff. Which was why I bothered with him at all. I don't socialize with punks, big or small.

So I grinned at worried, upset Benny and took each girl separately to one corner of the office. The three young ladies were named Lisa, Belle, and Sandy, and that was the only thing about them that was different. They were all brunette, long-legged, and had the same dull pretty faces.

I asked each of Benny's three sweethearts the identical question:

"How far apart are the runners of a toboggan?"

Lisa answered, "Five feet."

Belle squinted. "What's a toboggan? Some kind of foreign, fancy furniture?"

Sandy, honestly perplexed, answered, "Gee, I wouldn't know."

Benny was puzzled when I led Sandy to the door of the office and dismissed her. Then I turned back to Belle and Lisa. That time I asked the next question of both of them: "If you dial a Manhattan telephone number, how many times do you have to use your finger?"

Belle made a face and timidly asked, "Nine times?" But Lisa threw her head back and laughed, "Seven times, Stupid!"

Benny was even more confused when I asked Belle to join Sandy outside. Lisa was the only lady left and she began to look unhappy. I nodded at Benny Ricco.

"If one of the three did it, she's your girl, Benny. She's the only one smart enough and foxy enough to steal the combination of your wall safe as well as know how to use it."

Lisa started to call me all kinds of bad names, but Benny had already confiscated her purse and was emptying it on the desk. A small bankbook fell out and it developed that Miss Lisa had just deposited a large sum of money that very morning. So Benny had all the proof he needed. Lisa wailed that she'd turn the money back in, but Benny was through with her. You only cross men like him once. He was also very grateful to me to the tune of five hundred bucks. But he did want to know how I guessed Lisa was the guilty party.

If you've been reading carefully, the answer is clear enough.

Plain as Durante's nose, you might say. Right up front.

THE SOLUTION:

To the question, *"How far apart are the runners on a toboggan?"* Belle had claimed she'd never heard of a toboggan and she also didn't know about the Manhattan telephone dial — *it is seven digits* — which made her far too stupid to be able to work a complex wall safe combination. Sandy had said she didn't know just how far apart the runners were which made her far too honest a doll to try anything crooked. But the foxy Lisa had said, *"Five feet,"* which made her not honest and not too stupid not to try a guess, and led to her ultimate choice. Knowing the proper telephone dialings was the clincher.

The simple truth is that *there are no runners on a toboggan.*

There never were, there never will be.

Okay — let's try another puzzler.

See if you can answer the next one.

Riddle Three:
The Real Gone Horn

Reading Time: 4 minutes, 39 seconds

Hint:
Never go to a pawnshop.

Now, remember. The clue that's the key to the crime is there. See if you can spot it when I did so we can both find the answer for The Windup. As they say in the music field, let's take this one from the top.

Toots Kelly was missing again.

His rich Park Avenue wife, Babs, paid me two thousand dollars to find him for her.

They were quite a famous couple. Made all the headlines. Kelly, with his hot Dixieland trumpet, was one of the most promising musicians in the country until he started hitting the bottle. Then he started hitting his wife and their marriage mess-up made all the scandal rags and mags of the day sell like hotcakes. But Babs Kelly loved Toots — or so she said. And now he had run out on her again. Enter Ed Noon, Missing Persons Expert.

She wanted to find him before he really hit Skid Row.

I took the case.

I did it by the numbers.

I targeted in on all the nightclubs and side street cafes. Even Strip Row. But the managers of all those places all told me they'd never hire a drunken, unreliable bum like Kelly no matter how great a horn man he was. But finally the owner of the Blue Parrot opened up for me:

"Kelly? You'll find him drowning his sorrows with a nightclub dancer named Lola, who's always wanted him just for herself. Well, she finally got him, drunk as a skunk, but he's staying with her now."

Sure enough, I crashed Lola Lamont's dressing room at the Hot Angel on West Fifty-second Street, and there was Toots Kelly. Knee-deep in empty bottles of rye, sleeping a real binge off on a cot in the rear of the room. Lola, a six-foot blonde, put up quite a fuss when I butted in on her private life. She insisted Toots Kelly needed her, wanted her, and *that no-good, rich, ritzy dame is ruining him —* " I insisted just as hard that the man belonged with his wife, fed him a gallon of black coffee, and told him I was taking him home to Nyack where he belonged.

But he wouldn't go without his trumpet — his favorite horn.

Lola was so fed up by this time that she screamed at both of us — a sober private eye and a drunken lover — "You rotten fink, Toots! You pawned the horn yesterday to buy some of that lousy giggle-water — don't you even remember that? Here — !"

She flung an oblong yellow claim ticket in both our faces.

I had my job to do. I did it. I took the bleary-eyed, hungover Toots Kelly back to Nyack in my own Buick. There, a tearful Babs Kelly, waiting up for us, fell into his arms. But they were starting to argue all over again as I backed out of the fancy driveway and headed for the Turnpike.

The morning papers gave me an electric jolt the next morning.

Babs Kelly was dead.

Murdered.

Her lovely head bashed in with the famous Toots Kelly trumpet, and worse, far worse, the police had pinned the murder on Toots. That really jarred me so I went down to Headquarters where Captain Mike Monks let me talk to the man whose life, professional and personal, was going down the drain.

Kelly was in tears, hangover and all.

"I didn't kill her, Noon — I couldn't have — I loved her — "

"Sure you did," I said. "Take it easy."

18

"But if I didn't — who did — ?"

I left him like that and back in Monks's office, I checked over the inventory of items emptied from Toots Kelly's pockets. My old friend Monks let me take the pawn ticket without a whimper. We have worked on many a successful case in the past. I told him I'd be back with something worthwhile before the day was out.

I went to the pawnshop where the music-minded clerk on duty was amazed with the murder. He was equally amazed about the pawn ticket because he claimed that Toots had only redeemed the trumpet the week before. I thanked him and got out of there as he began to discuss the merits of the *Chicago* group.

I looked up Lola Lamont again.

I was waiting for her in the dressing room when she finished her last number — something with fans, a parakeet, and light bulbs. She sneered at me when she saw me.

"Haven't you done enough, Nosey? What else do you want from me? You took my man away and now he's up for murder!"

"I wanted to ask you about this pawn ticket."

I held it up so she could see it.

She shrugged, helplessly. "Only goes to show you, gumshoe. A guy hits the bottle the way Toots does, he'll do anything. Even hock his horn. His bread-and-butter. Then he doesn't remember doing it and ends up wondering where he lost it —— "

"I don't buy that, Lola. Toots was drunk, all right. He forgot things, sure. But he couldn't kill anybody. Not Toots Kelly, especially when he's drunk. He can hardly stand when he's loaded but — "

She turned from the mirror, where she was wiping her make-up off with cold cream. "Go on. What are you getting at?"

"Toots Kelly would not only not kill anybody, he wouldn't kill them with his trumpet — he couldn't have, *as a matter of fact*. But you could, Lola, and you did. Last night. You knew the lawyers could make a good case for Toots and you were willing to wait for him if and when he got out. Nice try all around, Lola, but you made a couple of mistakes. Better luck next time."

For an answer, she turned, a pearl-handled .22 revolver jutting from her hand. But I'd been ready for that. I knew she was a killer when I came in. I shot my own chair at her, she squeaked, tried to get out of the way. I was on her in a second, twisting the gun away from her hand before she hurt one of us with it. She suddenly started to cry, blubbering up at me, and between the tears she wanted to know where she had slipped up. I told her before I phoned Headquarters and Captain Monks.

You ought to have been able to answer that question too.

From the top.

THE SOLUTION:

Famous musicians have only *one* instrument.

The favorite one.

They may change a mouthpiece now and then, if it's a horn, let's say, but who ever heard of a Glenn Miller with two slide trombones or a Presley with two guitars? It's like Bergen and McCarthy, or the one and only puppets on *Sesame Street*.

So — Toots Kelly's trumpet could only have been at the estate in Nyack if *Lola had brought it there*. She admitted, under questioning, that she staged the pawn ticket scene to keep Kelly's horn as a sentimental keepsake, knowing he didn't remember anything so well anymore. But after I'd taken him home, she went out to Nyack to beg Babs Kelly to give him up. Kelly had been sleeping in the living room during the deadly argument between the two women in his life. A real gone man, all right . . . he would have been gone too — if I hadn't wound up his wife's murder. . . .

Well, how did you do on that one?

Let's try another.

Sorry, this time we have to go to the dentist's.

Riddle Four:
The Fatal Filling

Reading Time: 4 minutes, 40 seconds

Hint:
Visit your dentist twice a year.

Hi, it's Noon again. I'm the private eye and you're the Watson once more. Let's try again. See if you can solve this one before I give you the answer.

I had a tooth filled once and it very nearly killed me. Let me tell you about it.

John Fleming, a highly successful lawyer, was found dead, seated at the mahogany desk in his deluxe office. John Fleming had died of *curare*, a rare South American poison, and the cops had looked no further than his financial partner, Stanton Cobb. Cobb was a big game-hunter who had abandoned a law practice that ran into millions to run off to jungle land to mix it with the lions and elephants whenever he got the notion. Fleming had run the business for them both — beautifully — and the partnership had thrived like mad until a woman came on the scene. Fleming and Cobb had both loved the renowned fashion designer, Amanda Jeffries, and it was no secret that Fleming had won her favor hands down. The marriage had been only a month away when Mr. Fleming stopped swallowing. *Curare* can do that to you, quick as a bunny changing holes. What with *cherchez la femme* and *curare* both being things a Great White Hunter would know all about, the police were satisfied. They picked up Stanton Cobb and hung Murder One around his neck.

The trial was not too far off when Cobb's lawyer got in touch with me. He'd heard of the famous Ed Noon, and for ten thousand dollars he wanted all my time to uncover some new evidence that would prove *"Stanton didn't do it!"*

I said okay and went to work.

I visited the Cobb-Fleming law offices on Madison Avenue, and the personal secretary, Miss Simms, was glad to cooperate. She gave me a full list of John Fleming's itinerary on the day he was found murdered.

"It was five P.M. exactly when I walked in to say goodnight to him, Mr. Noon. He was sitting there — stone cold dead."

"Corpses can't move, Miss Simms," I said, gently enough. "Is there anything else you remember — something unusual?"

"Well, he'd been complaining only a few minutes earlier he hadn't been feeling well. That was before I walked in on him. He did look kind of pale — that mean anything, Mr. Noon?"

I said no and checked Fleming's appointment pad for that day. Fleming had interviewed a client on Madison Avenue by calling on him personally. That struck me as kind of curious. Big wheels like John Fleming don't go door-to-door to drum up new business. Miss Simms furnished me with the records of the firm of Fleming and Cobb, Inc. I read those records on the taxi ride down to Fleming's last client. The sheets in my hands only proved what everyone knew. Fleming and Cobb were fine for each other as partners and had equal shares in the firm. Not much there.

So I asked the last client — Klein and Farley — why John Fleming had gone down in person to see them. The partners laughed at that and explained how Fleming was really killing two birds with one stone. His dentist lived just around the corner and he had needed a filling, so he was combining businesses of that day.

"Did he go to the dentist first," I asked, "or see you two right off the bat?"

"No, Mr. Noon," Klein, the friendlier partner, replied. "When he left here, he was going straight to Dr. Maxwell. Why? Is that important? You make it sound highly crucial."

"Maybe so. Thanks, men. See you around."

Dr. Maxwell's office was hardly a block away.

I walked in, pretended an emergency, told him a molar was acting up and could he relieve my suffering? He waived aside the usual appointment nonsense and sat me down in his elegant, upholstered patient's chair. Fact is, I'd been meaning to have that tooth filled for months.

"We have a mutual friend, Dr. Maxwell. Darn shame about John Fleming, though. Dying like that. A rare poison, can you beat it?"

"Oh?" He wore glasses, Dr. Maxwell did, so I couldn't read his eyes. "You knew John Fleming, Mr. Noon?"

"Sure. I'm a private detective and I've been asked to see what I can find out about the murder. Of course, the cops think his partner, Cobb, is the man. But not me. I'm looking for a third party — "

"No more talking, Mr. Noon," Dr. Maxwell chuckled. "It's time for some drilling. But what you say *is* interesting —— "

My chattering might have made Dr. Maxwell nervous because he spent an awful long time drilling that tooth. He even scraped the inside of my cheek close to the filling, with his pick. When he asked me to spit out in the porcelain sink,

I kept on talking about the case and how a woman could louse up two good men. As he molded a silver filling into shape behind me, I could hear him clattering around. Finally, the job was done. I paid him in cash and left.

Downstairs I hopped into the nearest phone booth, called Captain Mike Monks at Headquarters, and told him to hurry on over with a police surgeon. I asked him to bring a stomach pump too.

I was pretty certain I had my murderer and knew now how John Fleming had died. But I wanted witnesses and the evidence intact, before I asked Monks to arrest Dr. Maxwell for the cold-blooded murder of John Fleming.

You ought to know how it was done too.

You were there with me.

THE SOLUTION:

The police surgeon cleaned out my tooth in the washroom of a nearby bar and pumped out my stomach just to play it safe too.

Dr. Maxwell's silver filling was a compact wad of *curare* with a fine gelatin cap which would have dissolved soon enough in the normal heat of my mouth to release the killing fluid. The poison would enter my system through the open cut on the inside of my cheek. *Curare* needs a wound to work on.

Dr. Maxwell had killed John Fleming because he was in love with Amanda Jeffries too, and would have been her choice if John Fleming had not come into the picture.

The murder method was foolproof because it was so brand new, and he had tried it on me in desperation because I had panicked him into it what with showing up and chattering about coming close to a solution. Love and passion makes even the smartest killers blind in a tight spot. I had a bad ten minutes testing my theory but I was still there for *The Wind-up*. Thirty-two teeth and all.

You really have to sink them into some of these cases, at times.

No matter how hard it is to digest them, sometimes.

Riddle Five:
Who Would Kill Ada Ven?

Reading Time: 4 minutes, 43 seconds

Hint:
<u>NOON</u> spelled backward is still <u>NOON</u>.

Come on with me, out to the Jersey wilds. A madman is threatening the life of a lovely Dancing Queen. We can stop him if we pick up the one clue that will spell The End for him. And this one we have to solve on the spot!

Sometimes a client is harder to get than a ticket for a long-running musical hit show on Broadway. Much harder. Then one day you're sitting around the office making paper airplanes and the phone rings. This phone call was a lulu. A show-stopper, you might say.

It was from Lee Simpson who ran a modern dance theater in Union City across the river. He wanted to see me right away.

"What's up, Lee?"

"Noon, some crank has been mailing threatening letters to my star attraction, Miss Ada Ven. I've notified the Law, of course, but I'd feel a lot better if you bodyguarded Ada until this crackpot is caught. What do you say?"

"I'm on my way."

I got over to Jersey as fast as the jalopy

32

would take me, and looked up Lee in his tiny office at the rear of the Emerald Theatre. Simpson was glad to see me and introduced me to Miss Ada Ven. In person. She was a statuesque six-foot giant of rounding curves. She showed me a stack of letters all postmarked New York. The tone of the mail was all fairly blue-nose, describing her performance as "low," "*degrading to womankind*," and all that stuff. There was also the touching reminder — that was in the very last letter mailed — that "*. . . if you dare to perform your disgusting exhibition on the night of July 22nd, I will shoot you down like the dog you are!*"

Ada Ven was pale under her garish make-up . . . understandably. This was the night of July the 22nd.

"Take it easy, Miss Ven. I've brought my .45 along to keep me company, and I'll keep a good eye on you from my box seat. The one that is closest to the stage. You do your show. I'll see there are no interruptions." She relaxed when I said that and told me a little about herself. As usual, the dancer-with-the-heart-of-gold.

She was an orphan, never mixed with any man, was putting two kid sisters through Life, and didn't know how she could have an enemy in the whole wide world. She also assured me that her dance act was not *dirty*, but the purest form of interpretive dance art. Lee Simpson agreed with her completely. But when Ada left to get into her costume for her big number, I checked Ada Ven out with him, anyway.

"She's aces, Noon. One of the best dancers in the business. The letter must just be some crank, mad at the world in general, but I can't risk Ada's life on that theory. Know what I mean?"

"I know. Excuse me, Lee. I want to go and see the show."

Sitting in my box seat while the music blared, I thought about what Lee Simpson had said. But I was all too familiar with show business tactics and he wouldn't have been the first businessman to whip up a sensation to juice up the box office receipts. Customers like thrills, and the Ada Ven-Crank Letter story had been all over the Jersey papers. It was terrific publicity and the packed house indicated that everyone in the Emerald Theatre wanted an eyewitness version of any real threat on Ada Ven's life. Come what may.

The pit orchestra went into the music of *Nevada* and Ada Ven danced from the wings to a deafening applause. I un-holstered my .45 in the dimmed theater and waited. I wasn't watching her at all. My eyes were pinned on the first five rows of the orchestra section and the balconies across from me. If anybody was going to shoot anybody on that stage, it was going to have to be from up close for any accuracy at all. Ada Ven danced and the audience went wild because she was very good. I was waiting for the finale where she spun like a top in a whirling dervish windup. It made you dizzy just watching her, and then it hit me. The whole thing. The solution, as it were.

So I stood up in my balcony seat, cupped my hands and yelled, as loud as I could, so that everyone in the Emerald must have heard me:

"GET OFF THAT STAGE! YOU'RE A DISGRACE TO THE FAIR STATE OF NEVADA! NO NEVADA WOMAN WOULD DANCE THAT WAY!"

I've got a loud voice. A very loud voice.

The orchestra, which had been playing low, jarred to a halt. Ada Ven stood shocked for a full second, then rushed off the stage in tears, clutching her lacy clothing in sudden fear. All eyes swung up to me and I could see several blue uniforms now charging in my direction. But what was better, far, far better: Some maniac jumped to his feet into the long aisle downstairs and started blasting away at the now empty stage with a big pistol, screaming, practically the same words I had used so melodramatically. He really sounded crazy.

The cops descended on him like a ton of bricks.

He was still screaming when they led him away.

Lee Simpson was overjoyed with my detective work because the guy's handwriting tallied with the horrible letters Ada Ven had been getting in her mailbox. But just like the cops, he couldn't guess where my wild hunch had come from. The on-the-spot trick which had flushed a madman and a would-be killer. To save a lovely dancer's life.

Can you?

THE SOLUTION:

Hunch it was — but it paid off.

Fanatics are always writing crank notes and Ada Ven's theme music had set me thinking. *Nevada* — a hit song back during World War II. *Ada Ven* spelled backward is *Nevada*, which couldn't be a coincidence. So some nut from her home town could conceivably have taken her act as a personal affront to the fair state of Nevada.

Whether he would have killed or not is a moot point, one Ada Ven had no desire to test. Neither had Lee Simpson or myself. Or the Law.

Well, there it is. A key clue again, acted on in a hurry — and it worked.

Not exactly Sherlock Holmes deduction or Edgar Allan Poe logic to solve a crime but ——

Anything that saves a human life is worth trying.

In my book.

Riddle Six:

The Dead Secretary

Reading Time: 4 minutes, 31 seconds

Hint:

Don't lick 'em and don't join 'em.

Crime after crime, the clock strikes murder. Sit in again with me on this one. I want you in on **The Windup** this time. This is a personal beef and I need all the help I can get. Keep your eyes peeled.

Being a private operator is a funny job.

You usually get hired for a fee by complete strangers to do their jobs for them and that's that. Fine. Just the way you want it. But every now and then you get personally involved and the case becomes different somehow. It hurts a little and clouds your thinking. Like the caper where I was dating Polly Thorne, a doll-faced secretary for a Madison Avenue export firm. She was quite a woman.

A real sweetheart with a great sense of humor. We got along famously. But one bright day she didn't show up for her job and when I checked out why, I got a real dose of the blues. The worst kind.

Polly Thorne was dead.

She had been sitting at her desk sealing a stack of first-class mail when she'd suddenly keeled over and died. Her two bosses, Paul Sweeney and Tom Adams, had rushed her to a hospital, but the first few seconds had been fatal. A heart attack. Polly Thorne was only twenty-six. Far too young for anybody to cash in her chips.

I felt bad about it, of course, and as the police were satisfied, there was no reason to doubt all the evidence.

But like I say, this was a personal thing and I had to be sure.

On some of our dates, Polly had idly remarked a couple of times about how fishy her firm seemed to be. I started remembering her comments about how Mr. Sweeney was always coming and going, to and from the office, with large suitcases. And how Tom Adams was such a stinker for making a lot of long-distance telephone calls to places like South America and London, England. Polly didn't like the brainwork of always making the connections with the local operator.

Nothing too odd in any of that, sure, but Polly Thorne had been my friend. Maybe my girl if I had had time to know her long enough. And now she was strangely dead at an early age. So I investigated. I *am* a detective.

She had been a lazy sort of female, who took her time about details and all things, never rushing herself, but I worked fast in her behalf. As if her ghost was pushing me from the graveyard.

I called on Sweeney and Adams, pretending to be a New York State Tax man who wanted to see their books and accounts and ledgers. All they did was get indignant when I couldn't produce any official papers or documents to back that up. In fact, Paul Sweeney, the bigger of the two, tried to use some muscle on me but I side-stepped him and poked him in the stomach before he could land a punch. Adams ordered me out of the office in a huff and I went. But not before getting a good long look at Polly Thorne's now empty desk where she was no longer sitting. The first-class envelopes were still stacked as she had left them. There was a large sheet of postage stamps with the top row missing. I also had time to look around for the porcelain moistener or sponge job that Polly would have used to wet the backs of so many stamps. There was none in sight. Weird that the first-class envelopes had not been mailed out yet, death of a secretary or not. Business still has to go on as usual, no matter what. Yes?

"Mr. Sweeney, friend, dear Mr. Adams," I told both of the loudly protesting partners, "I'll be back in roughly twenty minutes with more blue uniforms than you've seen since the Macy's Day Parade. I do want to see those books and your not wanting to show them shows me that you have something to hide. That ought to be good enough for John Law to make an investigation. Search and Seizure, maybe?"

"Get out!" Sweeney bellowed, bunching his fists. Adams growled too. But I got out, raced down to the lobby in a fast elevator, phoned Mike Monks of Homicide, and stuck my neck all the way out, making charges against Sweeney and Adams. Still, Monks owed me a favor and I owed it to Polly Thorne. I didn't like Mr. Sweeney and Mr. Adams, anyway.

Some twenty minutes after all that, Sweeney and Adams both came out of that same elevator, carrying about four suitcases. Monks and his squad of plainclothesmen, who had arrived a scant few minutes before, closed in on them from four sides of the lobby. Sweeney and Adams dropped their luggage and tried to make a break for it. I had the distinct pleasure of tripping up Sweeney so that he sprawled headlong to the tiled floor. For Tom Adams, I had a right to the jaw that had pure anger and satisfaction in it. Monks and his men did the rest. The handcuffs bit.

On the long ride to Headquarters, Sweeney and Adams screamed about their rights and wanting lawyers and phone calls, but I hinted that Polly Thorne had told me plenty before she died. They clammed up after that. They had to. They had been caught with the jam on their faces.

When we opened the four suitcases down at Headquarters, we found enough liters of heroin to fill a thousand hospitals with addicts. Monks was really pleased with my calling him in on the case, because if there is anything he hates worse than a dope salesman, it's *two* dope salesmen.

Now I knew why Polly had died, and I thought I knew how.

I asked Monks for permission to have a *post-mortem* performed on the body. A real autopsy this time, looking for something *un-natural*, something beyond a heart attack. There was enough justification now for the Law to assume Foul Play and that was enough for Captain Monks. And Polly had no known living relatives to contest such an action.

It was done and the coroner's report came in.

Sweeney and Adams now had a murder rap hanging over their heads — to add to their miserable record of narcotics-pushing.

And I felt real good about not letting Polly Thorne's death go unchallenged. Polly Thorne had been callously murdered.

With a rare type of deadly drug that assumed all the symptoms of heart failure.

If you've been on your toes, you know how the poison was administered too.

Don't you?

THE SOLUTION:

Lazy Polly Thorne would be just the type of secretary to lick stamps before affixing them to envelopes. *By her own tongue;* the absence of a moistener of any kind, porcelain, sponge, *etcetera*, convinced me of that since most office secretaries buy their own supplies for the place where they work. Sweeney or Adams, or both, had placed enough poison on the back of one of the stamps on the large sheet, in the top row, to ensure her death. But they had also arranged for their own death in the hot seat — by direct mail. Not mailing the envelopes off right away was a very large boo-boo, too.

All because they thought a secretary was a woman who knew too much.

What they didn't know was that she knew me.

The most restless private detective in the business.

Well, there's another one for you.

The Windup again.

Care to try another?

Riddle Seven:
The Cop Dodge Game

Reading Time: 4 minutes, 5 seconds

Hint:
How High Is Up?

This one was a humdinger. Totally un-expected, you might say. In fact, it came to me in the dead of night. So don't let it catch you napping, as it almost did me. You should never forget anything that you <u>know.</u>

Some cases walk into my office unan-nounced.

Other cases I walk into. Or blunder into like a bull in a china shop. Like the one last week which I want to tell you about. Funny thing, the bulls are in-volved too —— *bull* — that old expres-sion for a policeman or police officer.

I had just come from the bright lights of Times Square and Forty-second Street, where to kill some time I'd seen the poor remake of *King Kong*, and was on my way back to the mouse auditorium. The place I call my business office and second home.

But to reach my Fifty-sixth Street Shangri-La I decided to stroll through Columbus Circle and cut through Central Park for a pleasant midnight stroll. Which was when I saw this young woman in a silver fox fur coat being jumped by two mugs who pulled up in a dark blue Oldsmobile. It was the wee small hours of the morning and mugging is a common enough practice in Manhattan. But I moved quickly, anyway.

I dug out my .45 and scampered toward the little mob scene, as fast as my size nine shoes could carry me.

The woman in the fur coat was putting up quite a fight. She was clawing and scratching now and the street lights caught the thousand reflections of her white wrists which seemed to be loaded down with expensive jewelry. One of the muggers was behind her and had muzzled her mouth so she couldn't break through the sound barrier with a scream. His partner was methodically stripping the lady's wrists, but she was fighting so hard he had decided to blackjack her. The billy had just cleared his hip pocket when I reached them.

The barrel of my .45 came down on his skull and he let her go and hit the sidewalk with a noisy sprawl. His lousy partner came around the squirming woman and went for me with a knife that looked longer than my right arm. I didn't wait to introduce myself. I shoved my gun hand into his chin and he went down too.

Just then, the woman got her breath back and let go with a shrill cry of terror. On the sound, a beat cop showed up from literally nowhere, demanding to know what was going on. He was short on size but loud on authority, his head barely reaching my chin.

"Hey — what's going on here? — who are you, Mister? —— "

I put my gun away and flashed my P.I. license at him and he calmed down. But the woman didn't. All her fright had now solidified into hysterics. "Oh — why did I send my chauffeur home? — I wanted to walk — I could have been killed — if it wasn't for this man I would have — oh, Officer — what's happened to this city of ours —— ?"

The cop thanked me for my assistance but advised me to move along, that he'd handle everything by phoning his precinct station from a nearby call box. The two plug-uglies were coming to now, but the bantam-sized patrolman looked capable enough to handle them all by his lonesome. I said okay and moved off, ignoring the woman's loud and voluble *thank yous*. But once I was around the corner, out of sight, I jumped into the closest bar and dialed Headquarters myself. I gave them all the details in five seconds flat and got back to the corner as fast as I could. I craned my head just in time to see the tough cop helping the pair of muggers to their feet. The woman was nowhere in sight. But I could guess where she was. The dark blue Oldsmobile was still parked where it had been five yards from the scene of the crime.

I had a bad minute hoping I had done the right thing.

Pretty soon, I could hear a police siren wailing not far off in the night. The shrieking alarm ignited the cop and the still semi-conscious punks into furious action. They scrambled for the parked Oldsmobile. But I was ready for them, then.

I opened up from the protective covering of the wall.

My first shot sent the cop's pistol skittering from his damaged hand. Before the pair of would-be muggers could rouse themselves to action, I bounded out from the wall and covered them with the .45. Their startled, frightened faces were all the reward I would ever need.

"Okay, chums," I sang out. "A nice little racket you had here but it's come to a screaming halt. I suggest you spend a little more time learning the rules and regulations of the New York Police Department."

The wounded cop snarled, showing me an ugly expression.

"You lousy tinhorn — you had to butt in — rotten do-gooder — "

"Shut up," I said. "You'll have plenty of time where you're going to catch up on your reading. Hands high now. Till that squad car gets here. And no more lip from any of you. The lady might hear you."

The patrol car with the winking signal light came roaring up and the official people took over. The woman in the silver fox — rescued from the depths of the dark blue Oldsmobile — was properly grateful. She wrote me a four figure check that covered my expenses for this month and the next. And the next. The muggers had thought about kidnapping her.

How did I know the cop was a phony?

It was easy — if you know the rules and regulations.

Or anything at all about New York City.

THE SOLUTION:

To qualify as one of New York's Finest, you can't be one of New York's Shortest. Police regulations specify that to become a member of the N.Y.P.D., *an applicant can not be under five feet eight inches in height*. The beat cop had been a Mickey Rooney edition.

And also the brains of one of the shrewdest mugging con games that ever worked Manhattan after dark.

From *King Kong* to Mickey Rooney —

There's the ultimate for you. Both ends of the stick.

But it was *The Windup*, all the same.

Riddle Eight:

Bartree Has Escaped Today!

Reading Time: 4 minutes, 5 seconds

Hint:

**That's right — there is nothing left.
— Mother Hubbard.**

Manhunts are particularly absorbing. And when the man being hunted is the world's most dangerous killer, then you must be on your guard and ready for just about anything. If you can solve The Windup of this one, you belong to the Immortals of Detection.
To them — and with them.

Bartree had escaped.

Crashed out of Sing Sing day before yesterday. A man with murder in his soul and vengeance in his distorted mind.

Captain Michael Monks of the New York Police Department had alerted every manjack at his command to haul him in again. Public Enemy Number One — that was Bartree.

He had to be stopped before he killed his third man.

The first two were the Benzi brothers, two Italian shoemakers who had been brave enough to put up a struggle when Steve Bartree had tried to hold up their little shoe store on Third Avenue. One of the most savage double-murders in Manhattan police history.

And everyone knew who the third man was.

Judge Cyrus Sloane had pronounced the death penalty on Bartree. So with the electric chair staring him in the face, Bartree had busted out of the walled prison up at Ossining, the Ossining the cops had made famous by nicknaming it *Sing Sing*.

Nobody had to guess what Bartree would have in mind, now that he was roaming the streets, on the loose once more.

The day he had been sentenced to be electrocuted, he had leaped to his feet in the packed courtroom and made himself pretty clear.

In a shouting, terrible voice, his pointing finger leveled at the old gray-haired judge whose verdict had later been hailed all over the country:

"I'LL GET YOU, JUDGE, IF IT'S THE LAST THING I EVER DO!"

It seemed like an idle boast at the time, but now with the crazed killer free again, everybody seemed to remember his senseless, vicious gunning-down of the shoemaker brothers for a paltry eighteen dollars and fifty cents in the cash register.

When Captain Monks called me in to lend a hand with the case, I went along with him to Temple Courthouse where Judge Sloane was officiating that very day. Monks had thrown a squad of blue and plainclothes around the old building just on the chance that Bartree would try to cut the revered and wise judge down on the job. Monks figured that a twisted brain like Bartree's would operate on just such a notion. I was in complete agreement with him. "Ed, anything happens to the old man, I'm turning in my badge, so help me," Monks declared.

"No way," I replied. "If we can't stop that cuckoo bird — then we're both in the wrong business. Wait and see, Mike."

We sat in on the Judge's first case of the day.

Nothing happened.

The court was crowded as usual because the old arbiter was a real showman, with a flair for clean, incisive speech and sharp, plain decision-making. But now, with the added interest of a death threat hanging over him, he really was the center of attraction. The whole show. The only show.

Monks and I sat up front, close to the defending and prosecuting attorneys' chairs, where we could keep an eye on the judge, as well as all the surrounding people.

Everybody looked normal and natural enough. The human mob.

Men, women, a few teenagers, the bailiff, the patrolman on courthouse duty, the clerks — but we kept on trying to locate the ugly face of Bartree in that crowd of onlookers. I reasoned that Bartree would use a gun, if anything, and would have to work up close if he were to accomplish the mad deed, so I concentrated on the first three rows of seats. Quite a mixed bag of people there too.

There was a guy with a beard and a satchel in his lap who looked suspicious. Also, a pale man wearing huge sunglasses. A contradiction not easy to overlook under the circumstances. Then a rough-looking customer in a pin-striped suit just behind us who kept fidgeting noisily in his seat.

Monks had made the path clear for Bartree so he could be nailed again. But it *did* make a clay pigeon *and* a sitting duck out of Judge Cyrus Sloane. The old man knew it too, but he had guts and it was the way he wanted it. A woman just across the aisle from Monks and I, wearing a tan trenchcoat tightly buttoned on the right side, crossed her legs and stared intently up at the Judge. The bearded man suddenly coughed and the pale guy sneezed. I didn't wait a second longer.

Judge Sloane had just risen to his feet to declare a recess.

The moment held.

I vaulted over Mike Monks, sprang across the aisle and descended on the woman in the tan trenchcoat like a tree full of monkeys. The mad expression in her eyes was all I needed now.

I caught her flush on the chin with a hard-handed right cross just as her mitt was coming up from the folds of the coat with a wicked-looking Beretta pistol — the James Bond model. She went down and — *out*.

The courtroom was a riot scene as I tugged a blonde wig, putty make-up, and powdered false cheeks off the ugly face of Steve Bartree, the "woman in the tan trenchcoat." Whose other accessory was a murder gun.

Monks was overjoyed he had invited me in on the case.

But I'm no genius.

Bartree had made one mistake.

An elephantine one, all right, and it had cost him his freedom.

And delivered Judge Cyrus Sloane from the land of the Dead.

If I hadn't spotted the error, the old judge would be as lifeless as they can come, right this minute.

You must have eyeballed the colossal boner Bartree pulled too.

If not, here's what it was.

THE SOLUTION:

Bartree's disguise as a woman was great. Olivier might not have topped it. Except for one small error in reality. And judgment. And knowledge of things-as-they-are when it comes to *Male vs. Female*.

Bartree had buttoned the trenchcoat *on the right side*.

Just like the man he was.

Women have been buttoning their outer garments *on the left side* since Coco Chanel was a toddler. And that's the last century, almost.

So you could say a killer's force-of-habit led to *The Windup* on this outing. And do you remember what W. R. Burnett had one of his characters in *The Asphalt Jungle* say?

"Crime is a left-handed form of human endeavor."

Maybe that just about says it all. Sums it up for keeps.

Anyway, it's a cinch that Steve Bartree never read that book.

Though he'll have plenty of time now — where he's gone.

If they have a copy in the prison library.

Riddle Nine:
The Fairfax Kill

Reading Time: 4 minutes, 39 seconds

Hint:
I will not excuse your dust, Sir.

**Money can be a curse when you don't
know what to do with it. Follow this
story very closely and see how the Rich
can sometimes abuse the gift of great
wealth. And try to spot the weak link
in the chain of murder, so you can be
in with me at The Windup.**

The Fairfax killing made all the papers.
It pushed the space flights and Ber-
muda Triangle disasters right off Page
One. I had more than a passing interest
because Old Man Fairfax, the suntan oil
king, was paying me ten thousand dollars
to find the person or persons unknown
who had bludgeoned his son to death.
The body had been found in the library
of the family estate in Larchmont, on the
rainy night of May the third. The police
had made very little progress or headway
in their investigation on the day when I
showed up to collect my retainer from
Old Man Fairfax. He also wanted me to
look over the scene of the crime.

The ornate library was as clean as a
whistle because the bloodstains on the

Persian rug and the murder weapon, a ton-heavy statuette, were all down at the Police Lab. Exhibits A and B.

But the old millionaire tearfully filled me in on the sad and gory details. Some of which I had gleaned from the newspapers.

"Richard Jr. had come home from a Broadway play, Mr. Noon. He sat down in this very room to read a good book when somebody — " the old man brushed at his eyes angrily, " — somebody crept up behind him and hit him with that infernal statuette! They told me the left side of his head had been crushed like a — walnut."

"What *is* the statuette exactly, sir?"

The old man sighed, regretfully. "One of a matching pair. Figurines of horses rearing. They served as bookends for those sets of theater and drama tomes Richard was fond of collecting. The police took them both for microscope study."

I nodded, remembering things about the Junior Fairfax that his father was not telling me. Richard Jr. was somewhat of a playboy with his father's millions, having paid through the nose to many bright young women of the chorus line to keep the family name out of the scandal sheets. Old Man Fairfax gave me a stack of glossy photos and the corresponding names of ladies with whom Junior had been too familiar. The Senior Fairfax was certain, however, that one of them had killed his son in a jealous rage when she found out he wasn't "the marrying kind." All of the photos were inscribed to *"My darling"* and junk like that — so it looked like the old tycoon might be on the right track.

Then a maid came in to call the old man to the phone, and the poor old geezer tottered out. I turned my attention to the maid.

She was a petite but busty little thing named Mary Rogers, who had been with the Fairfax family for more than a year. Yes, it had been her night off when Junior was murdered. Yes, she recalled seeing the two horse-statuettes in their proper places when she cleaned up the library the night before. Old Man Fairfax had remained home that evening to the best of her knowledge — his bursitis was bothering him again so he had stayed in his upstairs master bedroom.

I believed her because of the tiny crucifix looped about her soft neck and the forthright way she answered all my questions.

"Did the old man and his son ever quarrel, Mary?"

"No more than any other boy and his father, sir."

I gave her a cigarette to put her at her ease and she took it with a delicate left hand. I walked over to the stack of theater tomes and volumes on drama, now no longer book-ended, and lying in sloppy disarray on an end table. There was a fine patina of dust lying over the mahogany top of the piece. I had no more questions but Mary Rogers very suddenly got a dizzy spell. She would have fainted and fallen to the floor if I hadn't caught her in time. Old Man Fairfax walked back into the library just then and his face opened in surprise. "See here, Mr. Noon! What the devil, Sir — ?"

"Sorry, Mr. Fairfax," I explained. "Mary got dizzy all of a sudden. Must be the closeness of this room. No windows opened since the night of the murder — you okay now, Mary?"

She nodded, catching her breath; the old man poured her a stiff shot of bourbon and her color returned. The old boy was a generous coot. He told her to take the rest of the day off and get some rest; things had been hectic what with the police running all over the house the past few days. She thanked him profusely and left.

Old Man Fairfax poured me some bourbon too, and swilled it around in his glass while he probed at his eyes with a veined, gnarled left hand. I looked at him closely because it always amazes me why some of us are detectives and others are not. He caught me staring at him and suspicion leaped from those old eyes for the first time. "You don't think — but good Lord, sir — that would be preposterous!"

Yes — that's right — it had been staring him right in the face since the night his son was murdered and he had not seen it.

"Yeah, Mr. Fairfax," I said, wearily, "I want Mary Rogers to submit to a blood test. If the answer is what I think it is, I know who killed your son and you owe me nine thousand dollars, seeing as how you have already paid me a retainer of one thousand."

I hope you have been able to see what I was getting at too.

It's all there, laid out right before your very eyes.

Clues, facts, tips galore.

THE SOLUTION: •

Junior Fairfax, being such a democratic Ladies' Man, could hardly have missed the tasty, eye-catching female named Mary Rogers who was a live-in maid at the Larchmont family estate.

Also, Mary Rogers was obviously a very religious young woman. How many young beauties have you met who wear the signs of their faith about their throats daily?

The blood test proved she was pregnant and according to Junior's record, he would never have approved of fatherhood or done the right thing by Mary. Mary Rogers' being left-handed confirmed the left angle of the smashing blow that killed Richard Fairfax Jr. while he was sitting reading a book. But the clue that set off on Mary Rogers' trail was the tiniest, possibly least important, clue to the entire crime.

The undusted books and table in the library only served to point up the very personal relationship of the maid in the life of the man who owned those books.

She just might have *hated to dust the books* of the man who was dusting her off so callously.

So she became the maid in the death of the man who owned those books.

Murder will out, at moments like that.

So will the character and personality of the murderer.

Ask any policeman.

Riddle Ten:

Inside-the-Park-Homicide

Reading Time: 4 minutes, 25 seconds

Hint:

Don't take me out to the ballgame!

You'd never expect to find the Grim Reaper listed in the boxscore of a baseball game, would you? But in my kind of business, Trouble and Death can be a double-play combination any day of the week. Batter Up and on your mark, Sherlocks. This is a tough one to handle. And as wicked as a line drive between shortstop and second base.

It was around the fifth inning of a Mets-Dodgers game at Shea Stadium, with the Metsies at the short end of a 7-2 score, when it happened. The guy sitting next to me in the lower grandstand seats suddenly doubled up like he had cramps and toppled face-forward. I helped him back to a sitting position, but by that time, the damage was done. His face had purpled magically and his tongue was twisting in his mouth.

I shouted to one of the beer-vending attendants to get a doctor. But while Kingman was blasting a bases-loaded homer to make the score 7-6, and the attendant was taking too much time to find a sawbones, the guy died. Right under my nose.

I went through his pockets for some clue to his identity as the fans sitting all around us buzzed with comment. I tried to remember something about the man who had sat next to me for five tense baseball innings.

He was fat and round like a basketball, with a big, bristly moustache that even now, in death, seemed charged with life and animation. I recalled how he had had a hot dog and several containers of beer because he had spilled some on my lap and apologized very nicely. Some cards in his wallet bore the name Carlo Santell, and he seemed to have been a rug dealer on Third Avenue since before they tore the elevated subway down. A park policeman arrived and tried to take over and restore some order among the excited crowd while I pitched in and helped. I bent down under the cushioned seats and rounded up the five empty containers under Santell's seat. He had liked his beer, all right. I sniffed at all of them like a bloodhound. I couldn't smell a thing. I asked the cop to find the hot dog vendor who I remembered as a tall, gangling kid with freckles. But a minute's questioning of the guy cancelled him out.

"You kidding, Mister? You know how many of these red-hots I sold today? You expect me to remember one customer with a big moustache? You must be crazy!"

He was right, of course. And I couldn't see how he could have affected the poisoning of one man. I forgot I was a Mets fan for the rest of that afternoon and went with the cop and the park doctor. Santell's body was removed to the nearest hospital.

When Captain Mike Monks of Homicide showed up two hours later, the Medical Examiner's report was in . . . and conclusive. Mr. Santell had died of arsenic poisoning. The next step was clear:

Notify the next of kin.

I went with Monks to a grubby little walk-up in the Village where his newly made widow lived. I got a mild surprise. Santell had been in his early sixties or more. His wife was a small, shapely, wide-eyed young thing who could not have been too long out of high school. She looked barely eighteen, if that. She collapsed when Monks broke the bad news to her. I walked into the bathroom to get some smelling salts or something to help revive her. Being the kind of eye I am, I explored the medicine cabinet while I was at it.

There was the usual toothpaste and shaving cream tubes and cold creams and deodorant bottles and other kinds of smell-water. But there was also a tiny brush I couldn't place for a minute. I sniffed it. And I figured it must have been left in alcohol at one time because it smelled like a brewery. Otherwise, it was stiff and fresh and as clean as a hound's tooth. There was also a small can of arsenic in that cabinet heavily labeled POISON in red ink, so there was no mistaking the contents. Lots of people use arsenic to kill rats and there are lots of rats in the Village. I took the can and the tiny brush and the smelling salts I had found back to the living room. Monks was having a hard time reviving Mr. Santell's distraught wife. Widow, that is.

I handed him the smelling salts.

"Wake her up, Mike," I commended him. "When she comes out of her swoon, I'm going to hit her with this." I showed him the strange little brush and the arsenic.

"What have you been up to, Ed?" he growled. "This woman was here all day. We proved that with her downstairs neighbor. She wasn't even at Shea Stadium. And that's where Santell was killed, wasn't it? You were right there yourself!"

I smiled my winning smile.

"It's true she wasn't at the ballpark, Mike. But she killed her husband as sure as Hank Aaron broke Babe Ruth's all-time home run record. And I am about to tell you just how she turned the trick."

You see, it wasn't difficult for me to dope the whole crime out once I remembered Mr. Santell's capacity for beer and just what kind of a man he was.

You ought to know too.

You were there with me.

THE SOLUTION:

Carlos Santell drank five containers of beer in five innings of baseball. Also, he had a big, bristly moustache, and mopping beer foam from it with the tongue is practically a *must* for moustachioed beer-drinkers.

The tiny brush from the medicine cabinet in the Santell apartment was a moustache brush. So it was a safe bet that dear little Mrs. Santell, probably stuck with a man old enough to be her grandfather, dutifully brushed her husband's moustache every day before he left the house. Big fat men love to be waited on, hand and foot. But the morning Mr. Santell had gone to the ball game, he hadn't guessed that his dear wife wasn't merely brushing his moustache that morning, loading the hairs with deadly arsenic — but brushing him out of her life forever. And out of this world. Knowing he would drink a lot of beer and lick the foam from his moustache, as he would have to.

See how easy it can be sometimes?

By the way, in case you care, the Mets finally won their game with the Dodgers that day.

Kranepool homered in the ninth with a man on to make it 9-7 Mets.

Riddle Eleven:
The Circus Catch

Reading Time: 4 minutes, 27 seconds

JOHN A. LESLIE
LIBRARY
SCARBOROUGH

Hint:

**The largest attraction in
The Greatest Show on Earth.**

Let's go to the Circus now. Plenty can happen under the Big Top that is never ever seen or understood by the millions who are in the audiences. There are the clowns and the artists and the animals. But there is also Tragedy, Terror, and Sudden Death. And sometimes, the biggest riddle of them all.

Barney Tell of Tomlin's Three-Ring Circus called me up three days after the terrible accident.

The police had been satisfied that it *was* an accident when Vern Rowles fell to his death in the middle ring at the Wednesday afternoon matinee performance at the Garden. Vern Rowles had made Big Top headlines with his phenomenal stunt of balancing himself on a seventy-five-foot pole, doing handstands and a whole kit of hanging and swinging acrobatics without the benefit of a net. But when the pole splintered close to the base and Vern Rowles plunged seventy-five feet to the hard floor of the arena, the shocking calamity made all the papers from coast to coast.

And now Barney Tell, Tomlin's manager, was calling in a private detective to go through the paces.

I saw Tell in his office on the circus grounds and he gave me all the information he had.

"Believe me, Noon, maybe all this is just what it seems, but bad blood can kill any circus, and if Rowles's death is anything but an accident I have to know that too. I've kept Tomlin's together for forty years. It's my whole life."

"What exactly do you want me to do, Mr. Tell?"

"Scout around. Look things over. I'll give you a thousand dollars if you can set my mind at ease."

"Make out a check, Mr. Tell. I'll be back."

I walked out of the office into the gigantic playing arena where a lot of the acts were rehearsing for that afternoon's show. If I was going to find out what really happened to Vern Rowles, I was in the right place. The circus playing area, itself.

My first stop was Ken Fremont who was putting his lions through their hoops. Fremont was a glib, burly guy in spangles, and when I flashed my badge he made no bones about his feelings for

Vern Rowles. In fact, he was downright emphatic about the dead acrobat.

"A real stinker that man, Noon. Mean, for no good reason. I caught him deviling my cats with an overdose of pepper in their meat at feeding time. I knocked him down for that one and no, I don't regret his accident at all. Couldn't have happened to a meaner guy. And you can quote me."

My next witness was Ben Argo, the elephant trainer. Argo backed up Fremont's story all the way. In fact, Argo went the lion tamer one better.

"Rowles," Ben Argo said grimly, "got some insane satisfaction in tormenting dumb animals. Know what he did once? Spread a load of hot coals in the sleeping quarters of my star elephant, Tillie. Poor Tillie. She went half-crazy, trumpeting around like mad until I watered her down. I never forgave Vern Rowles for that."

"Then you're glad he's dead too, is that it, Argo?"

Ben Argo squinted at me in a funny way.

"What do you think, Noon?"

As I moved around the big arena, questioning the roustabouts, I got the same story all down the line. Vern Rowles was a petty sadist and more than one of the acts had had trouble with him. Lila, the beautiful bareback rider of wild horses, admitted she had had a crush on Rowles until she caught him cruelly tugging the bit in her personal horse's mouth just to hear the dumb brute whinny. Well, I had heard enough by that time. Any one of a dozen suspects could have killed Vern Rowles, cheerfully. Nobody mourned him at all.

I went out to the big center pole where the accident had occurred. A new one, a towering shaft, thrust upward to the heart of the Big Top. But not far away, about five yards, I could see where the former pole had been. There was a jagged stump still rooted in the damp earth. I bent down to examine the thing.

The pole had obviously snapped near the base because the stump was no more than a foot high. The head of the stump was an irregular mass of chewed, jagged wood. It was a cinch it had not been sawed or cut or anything like that. It had literally snapped. Weakened to the point where it had simply splintered apart once Vern Rowles had reached the top of the pole. I got up and dusted myself off. The pole had been painted white at one time and the exposed stump had a huge scrape of some kind on it where the original color of the wood showed through. I was satisfied then because I had my answer. The easy solution, this time. I walked back to the office of Barney Tell, shaking my head. It's a mad, mad, mad, mad world all right. Sometimes, at any rate.

"Any luck, Noon?" Barney Tell asked me.

"Let me see the work roster, Mr. Tell."

He looked puzzled but handed me a huge clipboard with ruled sheets held down. I took a close look and found what I wanted. The clincher, that is. If I had any last doubts at all.

On the morning of the rehearsals, Ken Fremont's lions had worked in the same location with Ben Argo taking the spot right after he was done, with his priceless pachyderms. Lila, the bareback rider, had used the same ring too. The gang that hated Vern Rowles had all been there, as it were.

Ben Argo frowned. "Well, did you find anything at all?"

I folded my arms. "Forget this whole case, Mr. Tell. Vern Rowles was killed, all right. But you can't do a thing about it. And neither can the Law. This one will have to stay under the Big Top. A secret between you and me. You might say he got what was coming to him, anyway. If it didn't happen now, it would have happened sooner or later — "

"Noon," Barney Tell pleaded. "If you know he was killed then you know who the killer is!"

"I do," I agreed. "But no court in the land would convict this killer. And no jail on earth could hold him."

"Him?" Barney Tell echoed.

"Sorry," I said. "I meant her."

You ought to know who I was talking about.

If you have been following all this, carefully.

THE SOLUTION:

An elephant never forgets.

And Tillie, Ben Argo's prize peanut-eater, must have remembered the hot coals that Vern Rowles had carpeted her bed with on that mean day. Besides —

Only an elephant could have planted its big hoof right against the base of that towering seventy-five-foot pole on which Rowles performed his daily specialty. And moved its great weight to the point where the pole was weakened enough so that it just might break when Rowles went up there to do his stuff.

Yes, the paint scrape on that jagged stump matched the general imprint of Tillie's mammoth hoof. Left or right, it didn't matter. The damage had been done.

I was also certain the incident must have had a dozen witnesses. Who could miss what an elephant does in plain view?

But I was also certain that Vern Rowles had gotten exactly what was coming to him.

The A.S.P.C.A. wouldn't have batted an eye, either.

Riddle Twelve:

The Great Zampa Hoax

Reading Time: 4 minutes, 35 seconds

Hint:

Don't keep a secret under your hat.

Fortune-telling and seances, palm readers and tea leaf diviners are breeds apart. So be on your guard for this one. We are going to see a master magician in action. See if you can figure out wherein the magic really lies. And lies and lies and lies. . . .

I went with Theo Collins the night I saw the Great Zampa in action for the very first time. It was a unique experience from beginning to end. An eye-opener, you could say. The Great Zampa was a Showman, First Class. Never mind what else he was. That was my business, which was why I was there at all.

Normally, I'm not interested in swamis or crystal ball gazers or mystics who claim they can communicate with the graveyard. Theo Collins felt the same way but, unfortunately, her mother, rich, old Mrs. Collins, was paying a lot of money to the Great Zampa for just that. Zampa had promised to bring back the voice if not the face of dear, dead, departed Colonel Collins.

Theo had been just a long-legged kid

when the Colonel had cashed in his chips, and as much as she would have liked to see the old coot, she just didn't believe the Great Zampa could bring back the dead. In any condition. I didn't think so either.

Yes, Theo Collins was paying me a fat fee to prove the Great Zampa was a large fake. Old lady Collins would have been furious if she suspected that her beloved daughter had hired a private detective to check on her pet mystic. So, for that lone evening, I was posing as Theo Collins' boyfriend. Which was nice work, anyway. Theo Collins was gorgeous. And far, far lovelier than all of the thousand dollar bills she owned.

We arrived at the Great Zampa's stone house in the West Seventies at eight-thirty sharp. The proposed seance which would bring Colonel Collins back for a chat was at nine o'clock.

A gloomy-faced servant ushered us into the Seance Room where old lady Collins was already communicating a thick wad of bills to the Great Zampa himself. Theo snorted in disgust but she introduced me, without showing her true feelings about Zampa.

"Noon?" Mrs. Collins sniffed at me, expectantly. And the dark black eyes of the Great Zampa zeroed in on me, skeptically. "A rare name, sir. You are blessed by the stars and the Gods."

"Sometimes," I agreed. "What time does the show start?"

The Great Zampa was properly mysterious and Oriental in a swirling cloak and enormous turban crowning his dark, swarthy face.

We made a little more small talk and then it was nine on the button. The gloomy servant returned, solemnly drew the thick drapes on the windows of the room. Zampa motioned us to a circular deal table. I had already checked the place for trick wiring, hidden microphones, and phony lighting devices, and hadn't found any. The Great Zampa clapped his hands for silence and we all sat down. Just the four of us around that little table: Theo, Mrs. Collins, the Great Zampa, and yours truly, Ed Noon.

The room darkened so that we could not see each other very well. Zampa began to speak. In a low, droning, sleepwalker's voice. *"Colonel Collins. . . . Are you there? . . . We are gathered here . . . your loved ones . . . and I . . . Zampa . . . your friend . . . oh, Colonel. . . . We know you long to reach out and touch us. . . ."*

It was shivery, okay. No matter how much common sense you have or iron nerves you might own. Zampa was a spellbinder. His tone, his manner, all of it was masterfully calculated to produce the maximum effect on believers and unbelievers. ". . . *Colonel . . . speak.* . . ."

In that darkness, the faces about me were dim, pale, ghostly blurs. Zampa persisted with his pitch, telling the Colonel to come forward, make his presence known. That someone wanted to talk to him. We had all locked hands and Theo's slender fingers were cold in mine. Mrs. Collins' were like an icicle too. And then. . . .

The Great Zampa stopped talking.

And a thin, scratchy, reedy voice broke the silence.

Mrs. Collins gasped, Theo moaned, and the voice coming from a graveyard pitifully whimpered: ". . . *Mary . . . Theo . . . my babies . . . I have come . . . to talk to you.* . . ."

The old woman replied in a voice both shocked and delighted.

"Larry, Larry! Is it really you, my darling?"

"*Yessss . . .*" The incredible voice filtered back to us, as if from all directions . . . and no direction at all. ". . . *Mary*

. . . it's good to hear your voice again. . . ."
The deathly voice scratched on, but I had stopped listening. I was searching under the table because I have heard and sat through this kind of junk routine before. I carefully unlocked my hand from Theo's and placed it in the hand of her mother, withdrawing my other hand. Theo made a movement but she must have understood and said nothing. Mrs. Collins was too wrapped up in the Great Zampa's miracle to pay any attention to life around her. I eased from my chair in the gloom, moving toward the lights and snapped them on before anyone could stop me. The sudden effect was startling. Theo and Mrs. Collins screamed in fright and froze in their chairs. The Great Zampa, eyes closed, was leaning backward in a listening position, and what was crazier than that, Colonel Collins' dead voice was still talking. Only now, it was getting fainter and fainter.

Until it died in the new stillness, altogether.

Mrs. Collins sprang to her feet at that, calling me every name under the sun, shocking even her sophisticated young daughter with her bad language. Then Zampa came out of his trance, the dark eyes opened, blinking against the sudden light. His eyes held nothing but scorn and mockery for me. "Unbeliever . . . infidel . . ." he purred. "Spoiler of beauty . . . you have sent the dead away when they wanted to remain and talk with their loved ones. . . ."

"Shut up," I barked, "or I'll call you a few names myself. I don't buy this routine, I never have, and I never will — "

Suiting actions to my words, I raced around the Seance Room, turning over cushions, kicking drapes apart, pulling down canvases to look behind them. Without any luck at all. No wires, no record players, no man standing hidden somewhere doing the talking for the dead. I was starting to get embarrassed.

"Oh, Ed," Theo wailed. "Maybe it was true after all. . . ."

"Don't you believe it," I said. "Don't ever believe that."

The Great Zampa was beaming triumphantly, now ordering me to leave his sacred chambers. And then it came to me. How the trick was worked. How he had resurrected Colonel Lawrence Collins from the grave.

Without benefit of reincarnation.

And it had been staring me right in

the face since the moment I had first set eyes on the great charlatan and scoundrel.

Funny how nobody else had noticed it.

THE SOLUTION:

The enormous turban on the Great Zampa's head contained a tape recorder which was easily controlled by simple adjustments with the hand. The room being almost totally dark, nobody could have seen Zampa do his stuff. Manipulations and all.

The Colonel's voice had been easy enough to imitate and reproduce by any actor worth a nickel. He had been in enough old newsreels and TV talk shows for an enterprising phony like Zampa to make sure of his sound effects.

So Mrs. Collins didn't get her beloved husband back.

But she did get her money back and her feet back on solid ground. The dead cannot return — not ever. It's as basic as that. Believe anything else and you're in serious trouble.

Theo Collins was, of course, delighted in her choice of detective. The fat fee I was paid would have been reward enough.

Still, there were other bonuses in that case.

What's wrong with the fifth richest young woman in America being a fantastically beautiful creature who happens to think you are an All Right Guy, too?

Nothing, that's what.

See you around.

Riddle Thirteen:
The Last Weekend

Reading Time: 4 minutes, 22 seconds

Hint:
Beware of a sweet tooth.

Here's another riddle caper, under the five-minute limit. A mite unusual this time because it almost cost me my life. When you get too close to a killer, that can happen. Probably that's why you have to be so careful with the clues. E-specially when they point in only one direction — and it is where the killer is standing. Waiting to kill you.

Winding up the Scholditz Case was tough.

There were two big question marks, bigger even than Mount Everest or the Grand Canyon.

Who killed Harry Scholditz? And why?

And I was right smack in the middle again — *unconscious*.

That's right. When I came to, I was lying in a pool of blood. *My own blood*. Near the swimming pool in Marla Grange's spacious back yard. But a back yard unlike yours. With patios, bars, and mile-high trees bordering one of the fanciest layouts in the world.

Funny how events race through your mind when you're coming out of a deep sleep. The kind of sleep that starts with a bang. I'd been poking around for clues on the Grange estate when somebody poked me from behind. With a poker, of course. It felt just as heavy and just as ironlike.

Through the throbbing music of unconsciousness, I could see the whole fantastic weekend flash by in a matter of seconds. . . .

The beginning of it all was Marla Grange's house party.

The Marla Grange. The biggest, starriest actress on Broadway, the darling of the Big Apple. And the most scandalous female celebrity alive. With me, Ed Noon, hired and invited to hang around the premises, to keep the guests from socking each other or robbing each others' diamond necklaces and fabulous jewelry. And then Harry Scholditz had driven up from New York in his flashy Mercedes-Benz and joined the festivities. Harry had staggered out from behind the wheel, taken three steps onto the fancy green lawn, and then very quietly dropped dead. Dropped dead at Marla's expensive country place — a castle for upstate New York — about one hundred miles from civilization and Times Square. Far from Law and Order too.

When we reached Harry, he was beyond help.

The smell of bitter almonds on his lips was unmistakeable. He'd been poisoned. Self-induced, or what?

I found a box of chocolates in the glove compartment of the Mercedes. A pound box. It had been opened. One piece was missing. We all knew where that piece was. In Harry, of course.

Harry Scholditz had been famous for a sweet tooth. He had had a mania for anything chocolate-covered, besides.

The party was loaded with top-grade, first-rate suspects.

Besides being Marla Grange's agent, Harry Scholditz was her current beau, her preferred man — Number One in Marla's life. Therefore, the focus of envy and jealousy on the part of just about every man at the party.

A lot of Marla's famous ex-boyfriends were all over the place.

There was Johnny Jackson, the sweetheart before Scholditz. A jock who was an expert on horses. And Radcliffe, the surrealist painter who had once enjoyed her favors. As well as Ben Miller, a trumpet man who blew a mean horn. Not to mention Bob Browning, the writer who dedicated his last novel to Marla Grange. I could see they all still loved her and any one of them could have killed Harry, gladly.

Marla Grange was one of the most beautiful women I have ever seen. She knew it too, as did the entire world.

But she got rid of old flames faster than the New York Fire Department. One of the reasons her reputation wasn't so nice.

I took the candy box for evidence and was looking through it on a beach chair by the swimming pool. Everybody else was inside the house, making calls to say they would be delayed because the local law was investigating. That was when somebody conked me from behind. When I finally came out of it, the candy box was gone.

And so were Marla Grange and all the guests too!

But I knew what I had wanted to know.

The candy box was important . . . to the killer . . . or killers.

Somebody had sent it or given it to Harry Scholditz *who was supposed to eat the candy in New York*. And die in New York. Far, far from the murderer. Harry's turning up the way he had must have scared the guilty party silly. And everyone had taken a powder now before I or the local gendarmes could ask a lot of embarrassing questions.

But I didn't have to ask anybody anything.

I phoned Captain Monks of Homicide, asking him to issue an All-Points-Bulletin for a murderer who went in for the Poisoned Chocolates murder method. I had it cold now. The case, I mean.

The solution was there as plain as the lump on my skull.

It was *The Windup* again, and this time I hadn't had to work too hard at all. Except to take a pretty rough blow on the head.

But the knockout and the missing candy box had given me the answer to the murder of Harry Scholditz.

Just like that.

You ought to have the answer too, by this time.

THE SOLUTION:

Poison — the kind that smells like bitter almonds — works fast.

Which only means one thing.

Harry Scholditz had to have eaten the fatal piece of candy *while he was en route from New York to the Grange estate.* Somewhere along that one-hundred-mile stretch of roadway, he had poisoned himself. Unintentionally and accidentally, on his part.

The candy had been sent or given to him, and of course, he had been invited to Marla's party since he was the current favored man in her life. Knocking me out and disposing of the candy box pointed a finger right at the killer. For Harry certainly would not have eaten a chocolate from a box he was intending to bring Marla as a party gift. A dirty sticky finger of death — all because Harry's sweet tooth was such a famous legend — a known fact about him.

A finger that belonged, certainly, to Marla Grange.

Who, alas, was no longer wild about Harry.

Who wanted a private detective for an alibi.

Who knew more than anyone about Harry's sweet tooth.

Who had hoped he would crash somewhere on the highway, hiding her crime forever in some kind of flaming car wreck.

But *The Windup* ends as it always does.

With a lock-up . . . for Marla Grange — not a very nice woman at all.

Famous Riddles from All Over the World

1. How would you divide 13 apples equally among 12 people?

2. In a crowd of more than two hundred people, one man murders another and leaves the scene of the crime with the corpse, unseen and unapprehended. How is this possible?

3. She cost a fortune, more than a thousand men loved her, and she made every one of them older but not one was ever jealous or regretted his feelings for her. Who was she?

4. A deaf-mute couple had a violent argument in their bedroom. How did the husband end the argument?

5. Why was the box of writing paper on the desk not moving?

6. What has four wheels and flies?

7. Why do radio announcers have small hands?

8. What is the difference between a radio and a clothesline?

9. How does a gambler count?

Answers

1. By making applesauce.
2. The murder occurred at a drive-in movie.
3. The battleship, *USS Missouri*.
4. By turning out the lights.
5. Because it was stationery.
6. A garbage truck.
7. Wee paws for station identification.
8. A radio draws the waves and a clothesline waves the drawers.
9. One, two, three, four, five, six, seven, eight, nine, ten, jack, queen, king, ace.

Word Riddlers — Tricks with Talk

1. What is round on the end and high in the middle?
2. What is the longest word in the English language?
3. What has four eyes but cannot see?
4. What runs but has no legs or feet?

5. Where was the Declaration of Independence signed?

6. When is a door not a door?

7. What is the definition of illegal?

8. Why did they bury the crook on the side of the hill?

9. How far can you walk into a forest?

10. Where does the lion eat in the jungle?

11. What is black and white and read all over?

12. What goes 99 *Thump!* 99 *Thump!* 99 *Thump?*

Answers

JOHN A. LESLIE LIBRARY SCARBOROUGH

1. Ohio.

2. Rubber.

3. Mississippi.

4. A clock.

5. On the bottom.

6. When it's ajar.

7. A sick bird.

8. Because he wasn't on the level.

9. Halfway; the other half you're on your way out.

10. Anywhere he wants.

11. A newspaper.

12. A centipede with a wooden leg.